THE BREEZE THAT REVEALED HER BEAUTY

THE BREEZE BROUGHT HER TO ME

JAMES ROBERTS

Edited by
JAMES ROBERTS
Illustrated by
JAMES ROBERTS

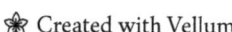

CONTENTS

INTRODUCTION

.

This book is a short story of Romance and Erotic Love enveloped in a Strange Reality. This is the second book by James Roberts outside the Julia Lillus Crime Series.

PREFACE

'I wasn't on this excursion for anything but relaxation. When I saw the beauty the breeze brought with it, I couldn't resist following through with thankfulness.'

THE EXCURSION

I had planned the excursion to visit the castle over the summer. My work has been very stressful, and I needed to get away for a while. I was told a castle nestled on an island, out on a great river, was a site to be seen since it hadn't been attended to for such a long time. Everyone said the renovations are spectacular.

The day arrived, and I readied myself to travel to a park where I was to take a shuttle boat to the grand castle. I took the time to relax a few days before embarking on the highlight of my vacation.

Stepping on the boat, I got a glimpse of the island and the turrets of the castle above the trees surrounding it.

The shuttle to the island lasted a full ten minutes and as I stepped off, I asked the attendant at what time the shuttle to the boathouse would take place. I opted to visit the boat house before touring the castle, for the boathouse was a castle in its own right.

The boats within the boathouse were circa early eighteen and nineteen hundreds and quite magnificent. Every boat there, named after a female, made sense to me seeing their beauty.

THE BREEZE

After my need to visit the boathouse was satiated, I again rode the shuttle back to the castle. At that point, I did not realize what lay ahead for me and would change my time there, immensely. I stepped off the boat as it landed at the dock below the castle grounds. I had pre-purchased my ticket for entrance, so I walked over to the ticket counter waiting to be ushered towards the castle entrance.

There is a steady, but warm breeze on this day in late September, although fall is well on its way. As I enter through the gate, I look down at my shoes noticing a lace is loose. I bend down to tie the lace. As I stand up, I notice out of the corner of my eye a girl of about twenty years of age walking towards the exit gate of the castle grounds. She has blonde hair, a cute face with just enough makeup to bring her true beauty to fruition. She is wearing a flowing dress, colored white and black with flower pastels throughout. I look forward through the entrance gate when a steady, but brief whisper of a breeze passes me by, and for a split second I see it lift the beauty's dress to her waist. She isn't wearing panties, and I see a very soft, slightly pink and plump cheeked hind-end. As her closed cheeks lead to where her legs meet her torso, the light pleasantly darkens the pink to soft shadows outlining the separation of her legs. She realizes with embarrassment and quickly pushes her dress down, hiding the beauty I just witnessed. As I look up, her eyes reveal I entered into her intimacy.

3

THE INVITATION

I continue my tour of the castle, but cannot get the view I had just seen out of my mind. Every time I close my eyes, I can see her beautiful, toned and inviting be-hind. I can't say that the image is ruining my castle tour, but I am not enjoying it as much had I not seen her. I realize I am entering a new drive; I no longer want to go back to the park and relax; I need to find this beauty. I cut my tour short and travel toward the exit, determined to search for her. I search the concessions with no luck. Just as I am ready to give up searching, I notice the back of the head of a female with blonde hair over on the shuttle boat. I quickly step onto the boat just as it is leaving the dock. There is room on the bench she is sitting on, so I settle myself next to her. I feel she knows I am the guy who had seen her intimacy under her dress; the feeling hit me from her facial expression. I can't help looking down at her knees, which are poking out from under her dress with enough thigh showing, leading my mind to look through her dress from under the bench, gazing at her beauty.

"Isn't the castle spectacular with the latest renovations?" I ask the beauty sitting next to me.

"Yes, quite spectacular," she replies.

"It is quite breezy and warm for a fall day."

"Yes, it is," she replies.

"Look, this is very difficult for me to divulge, but I am the guy who saw the breeze lift your dress."

"I know. I am so embarrassed," she replies.

"Oh, I am the one who should be embarrassed. I didn't mean to look. I was just standing up from tying my shoelace and it happened so fast."

"I am sorry," she replies.

"You needn't apologize. Hey look, my name is Jim, Jimmy Faust. How would you like to accompany me for dinner tonight? We can surely turn this into a laughing matter."

"I don't know. I hardly know you."

"Well…,"

"Beth, my name is Beth Ridley."

"Well, Beth, what a better time for us to get to know each other."

"Well, OK, but I will be leaving the area later tonight."

"No problem. How about making it an early one, say six this evening? Where can I pick you up?"

"You can pick me up at the docks on the mainland."

"Sure, Beth, see you at six."

THE TOUR

I travel back to my place of stay in the park and I cannot get the vision of her beautiful ass out of my mind. I am obsessing so much about it I am feeling I need to know more about what she is hiding from me under her dress.

"Hello, Beth. I was afraid you wouldn't show up."

"Why would you think that, Jim?"

"Well, with the embarrassment and all. Would you mind taking the night cruise back over to the castle having dinner on the shuttle? I hear they serve a wicked buffet."

"Sure, that would be splendid Jim."

"I purchased two tickets for the castle tour. Would you like to tour it with me, Beth?"

"Do you mean tonight? I have to leave later."

"What do you have to leave to, Beth?"

"I have to get back to my work."

"Oh, what do you do at your work?"

"I am in accounting at a very large firm in New York."

"Accounting? That is a pleasant job, Beth."

"Yes, I like it. And yes, I think I have time to take the tour with you, Jim."

5

LOCKED IN

"Jim, I think I left my purse in the castle ballroom and when the attendant started talking about the parties held there, I didn't think about it not being on my shoulder."

"I will go back and get it for you, Beth. Stay right here so I don't lose you."

Ladies and gentlemen, the castle will close in fifteen minutes. Please make your way to the exit. We will be open tomorrow at ten in the morning.

"Jim, I think they closed the castle!"

"I am sorry, Beth. I got lost getting back here."

"I don't hear anyone and haven't seen an attendant for a while. I think they locked us in," says Beth.

"Let's go check the entrance door, Beth."

"Just as I thought, Jim, they locked it. Now what do we do?"

"I guess we spend the night here, Beth."

"Where are we gong to sleep and oh no, my work! I won't get back there."

"How about you go up to the maid's quarters and make yourself at home in her bed? I will sleep here, in the parlor."

"Jim, I am afraid to be alone on the third floor; castles are spooky. Could you find a room up there to sleep in?"

"I am sure I can find something, Beth."

"Here is the maid's quarters and there is a room with a bed next to it for you," says Beth.

"Have a good sleep Beth and if you need anything, just knock on my door. I am not a heavy sleeper."

"Goodnight Jim."

THIS NIGHT IS SPECIAL

I am so close to her now. I have a bedroom right next to hers and she will lie under the covers, possibly nude, and I will be in the next room wishing I was in bed right next to her. My mind is racing and I just have to check on her. I quietly slip out of my bedroom door and head towards her bedroom door. I notice the door is slightly open and a glimmer of light from the full moon is casting light through the window. As I peer into her room, I see a silhouette of her standing in front of the window as the moon shine glows upon her nude body.

"Jim, is that you?"

"Yes, Beth, I was just checking on you."

"Jim, come in, please."

"I shouldn't Beth."

"Jim, you have seen my ass this afternoon. Wouldn't you like to see the rest of me?"

"Well, I…"

"Jim, we are all alone and being with you for just a short period of time, studying your thoughts, I am sure before dawn you will have made a home in my bed."

"Well, I…"

"I am correct in my thinking, Jim?"

"Well, I.."

"I might as well invite you to my bed. Come here to me and take a closer look at what I have to offer you."

"Beth, I don't think we should…"

"Jim, what were you thinking when the breeze lifted my dress this afternoon?"

"Well, I.."

"Jim, you wished you could see more; you wished you could explore what else I had under my dress? I know men, Jim."

"I guess you are correct, Beth."

"Place your arms around my waist and place your hands on my ass."

"Beth, you don't know what you are asking for."

"Jim, I do know what I am asking for. I am looking for a one-night stand with you and I want you to explore my body fully while I ready myself."

"Ready yourself for what, Beth?"

"Come on Jim, isn't it your intention to fuck me?"

"You might not like it, Beth. I am quite rough in handling a female."

"I can handle it, Jim. Now twist my nipples with your fingers and then place one of those fingers in my crease and massage; make me scream!"

"Beth, lay down on your stomach. I want to gaze at your ass I got a glimpse of. It is as soft as I envisioned."

"Slap me harder, Jim! Make my ass red with warmth!"

"Beth, I can no longer abstain!"

"Go ahead, spread my cheeks and sink that large cock of yours into me. Push hard, Jim, I want to feel you hit the end of my love tunnel."

"Quiet, Beth, I think I heard something."

"Jim, this isn't the time for us to be quiet."

"Shh..."

MR. ROCKNER

"Jim Faust, Jimmy, you need to wake up!"

"I don't want too."

"You have too. I just started," says Jim.

"Jim, you know the deal. Time is up and you have to come out of your dream."

"I want to re-negotiate the deal, Mr. Rockner," states Jim.

"You can't Jim. You will die," says Mr. Rockner.

"I will die then. I want to die in her arms."

"Jim, it was thirty years ago…"

"But you did it. The proof is here, right here!" exclaims Jim.

"Jim, you can't go further. Remember, there is 'no further' to go to."

"But I did go further."

THE DISCOVERY

"Jim, I think you are hearing things in this old castle."

"Beth, sit tight. Don't move from that position. I need to check it out."

"Hurry, Jim. We have been in foreplay most of the night and soon it will be dawn. We have to get to fucking!"

"Who the hell are you and how did you get in here?"

"My name is Jim Faust, and I didn't get out in time before they closed the doors and locked them: I spent the night. I have a ticket. I was touring the castle."

"I am the night watchman and no one is to be in the castle after touring hours."

"Sir, I tried to leave but they locked the doors."

"Are you the only one in the castle? Is there anyone with you?"

"No sir, I am the only one."

"Well, Jim, you look a little disheveled. Are you sure no one is here with you, like maybe a woman?"

"No sir, I am all alone. I wish there was a woman here, with me."

"I've been there. The hand is not as good as a warm and moist pussy."

"You got that right! Can I leave now?" asks Jim.

"Yes, and be sure to leave the next time there is a fifteen minute call on your next visit."

"Great, now I have to figure a way out of here. Thanks Jim for not including me. Now where are my clothes?" Beth asks herself.

I NEED TO GET BACK TO HER

"Mr. Rockner, isn't there a way? Are you sure?" asks Jim.

"It is very hard just to relive a dream, let alone add to the dream something that didn't happen."

"But something did happen. We can try, can't we?" asks Jim.

"No, I won't do it! It is way too risky!" exclaims Mr. Rockner.

I decided to not heed Mr. Rockner's advice and hole myself in my bedroom for a day thinking about Beth and her luscious ass. I draw pictures of what I can remember and the picture of her dress lifting that day, was so accurate and finely detailed; I felt if I could just push my hand into the picture, I would feel her bare ass and it would feel just the way I imagined it…no, I didn't place my hand on her ass…yes, I did…yes, I did..

 "Beth; the castle; the shuttle; the wind; the breeze; her dress lifting; her plump and perfect ass. Beth; the castle; the shuttle;

the wind; the breeze; her dress lifting; her plump and perfect ass. Beth; the castle; the shuttle; the wind; the breeze; her dress lifting; her plump and perfect ass. Beth; the castle; the shuttle; the wind; the breeze; her dress lifting; her plump and perfect ass. Beth; the castle; the shuttle; the wind; the breeze; her dress lifting; her plump and perfect ass..."

RE-LIVING THE DREAM

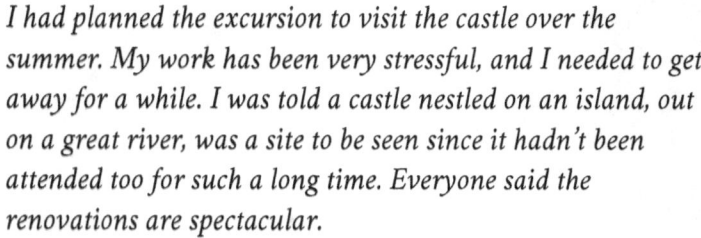

I had planned the excursion to visit the castle over the summer. My work has been very stressful, and I needed to get away for a while. I was told a castle nestled on an island, out on a great river, was a site to be seen since it hadn't been attended too for such a long time. Everyone said the renovations are spectacular.

The day arrived, and I readied myself to travel to a park where I was to take a shuttle boat to the grand castle. I took the time to relax a few days before embarking on the highlight of my vacation.

Stepping on the boat, I got a glimpse of the island and the turrets of the castle above the trees surrounding it.

The shuttle to the island lasted a full ten minutes and as I stepped off, I asked the attendant at what time the shuttle to the boathouse would take place. I opted to visit the boat house before touring the castle, for the boathouse was a castle in its own right.

The boats within the boathouse were circa early eighteen and nineteen hundreds and quite magnificent. Every boat there, named after a female, made sense to me seeing their beauty.

After my need to visit the boathouse was satiated, I again rode the shuttle back to the castle. At that point, I did not realize what lay ahead for me and would change my time there, immensely. I stepped off the boat as it landed at the dock below the castle grounds. I had pre-purchased my ticket for entrance, so I walked over to the ticket counter waiting to be ushered towards the castle entrance.

There is a steady, but warm breeze on this day in late September, although fall is well on its way. As I enter through the gate, I look down at my shoes noticing a lace is loose. I bend down to tie the lace. As I stand up, I notice out of the corner of my eye a girl of about twenty years of age walking towards the exit gate. She has blonde hair, a cute face with just enough makeup to bring her true beauty to fruition. She is wearing a flowing dress, colored white and black with flower pastels throughout. I look forward through the entrance gate when a steady, but brief breeze passes me by, and for a split second I see it lift the beauty's dress to her waist. She isn't wearing panties, and I see a very soft, slightly pink and plump cheeked hind-end. As her cheeks lead to where her legs meet her torso, the light pleasantly darkens from pink to soft shadows outlining the separation of her legs. She realizes with embarrassment and quickly pushes her dress down, hiding the beauty I just witnessed. I glance at her eyes revealing she knows I entered into her intimacy.

I continue my tour of the castle, but cannot get the view I had just seen out of my mind. Every time I close my eyes, I can see her beautiful, toned and inviting be-hind. I can't say that the image is ruining my castle tour, but I am not enjoying it as much had I not seen her. I realize I am entering a new drive; I no longer want to go back to the park and relax; I need to find this beauty. I cut my tour short and travel toward the exit, determined to search for her. I search the concessions with no luck. Just as I am ready to give up searching, I notice the back of the head of a female with blonde hair over on the shuttle boat. I quickly step onto the boat just as it is leaving the dock. There is room on the bench she is sitting on, so I settle myself next to her. I feel she knows I am the guy who had seen her intimacy under her dress; the feeling hit me from her facial expression. I can't help looking down at her knees, which are poking out from under her dress with enough thigh showing, leading my mind to look through her dress from under the bench, gazing at her beauty.

"Isn't the castle spectacular with the latest renovations?" I ask the beauty sitting next to me.

"Yes, quite spectacular," she replies.

"It is quite breezy and warm for a fall day."

"Yes, it is," she replies.

"Look, this is very difficult for me to divulge, but I am the guy who saw the breeze lift your dress."

"I know. I am so embarrassed," she replies.

"Oh, I am the one who should be embarrassed. I didn't mean to look. I was just standing up from tying my shoelace and it happened so fast."

"I am sorry," she replies.

"You needn't apologize. Hey look, my name is Jim, Jimmy

Faust. How would you like to accompany me for dinner tonight? We can surely turn this into a laughing matter."

"I don't know. I hardly know you."

"Well...,"

"Beth, my name is Beth Ridley."

"Well, Beth, what a better time for us to get to know each other."

"Well, OK, but I will be leaving the area later tonight."

"No problem. How about making it an early one, say six this evening? Where can I pick you up?"

"You can pick me up at the docks on the mainland."

"Sure, Beth, see you at six."

I travel back to my place of stay in the park and I cannot get the vision of her ass out of my mind. I am obsessing so much about it I am feeling I need to know more about what she is hiding from me under her dress.

"Hello, Beth. I was afraid you wouldn't show up."

"Why would you think that, Jim?"

"Well, with the embarrassment and all."

"Would you mind taking the night cruise back over to the castle having dinner on the shuttle? I hear they serve a wicked buffet."

"Sure, that would be splendid Jim."

"I purchased two tickets for the castle tour. Would you like to tour it with me, Beth?"

"Do you mean tonight? I have to leave later."

"What do you have to leave to, Beth?"

"I have to get back to my work."

"Oh, what do you do at your work?"

"I am in accounting at a very large firm in New York."

"Accounting? That is a pleasant job, Beth."

"Yes, I like it. And yes, I think I have time to *take the tour with you, Jim.*"

"Jim, I think I left my purse in the castle ballroom and when the attendant started talking about the parties held there, I didn't think about it not being on my shoulder."

"I will go back and get it for you, Beth. Stay right here so I don't lose you."

Ladies and gentlemen, the castle will close in fifteen minutes. Please make your way to the exit. We will be open tomorrow at ten in the morning.

"Jim, I think they closed the castle!"

"I am sorry, Beth. I got lost getting back here."

"I don't hear anyone and haven't seen an attendant for a while. I think they locked us in."

"Let's go check the entrance door, Beth."

"Just as I thought, Jim, they locked it. Now what do we do?"

"I guess we spend the night here, Beth."

"Where are we gong to sleep and oh no, my work! I won't get back there."

"How about you go up to the maid's quarters and make yourself at home in her bed? I will sleep here, in the parlor."

"Jim, I am afraid to be alone on the third floor; castles are spooky. Could you find a room up there to sleep in?"

"I am sure I can find something, Beth."

"Here is the maid's quarters and there is a room with a bed next to it for you," says Beth.

"Have a good sleep Beth and if you need anything, just knock on my door. I am not a heavy sleeper."

"Goodnight Jim."

I am so close to her now. I have a bedroom right next to hers and she will lie under the covers, possibly nude, and I will be in the next room wishing I was in bed right next to her. My mind is racing and I just have to check on her. I quietly slip out of my bedroom door and head towards her bedroom door. I notice the door is slightly open and a glimmer of light from the full moon is casting light through the window. As I peer into her room, I see a silhouette of her standing in front of the window as the moon shine glows upon her nude body.

"Jim, is that you?"

"Yes, Beth, I was just checking on you."

"Jim, come in, please."

"I shouldn't Beth."

"Jim, you have seen my ass this afternoon. Wouldn't you like to see the rest of me?"

"Well, I..."

"Jim, we are all alone and being with you for just a short period of time, studying your thoughts, I am sure before dawn you will have made a home in my bed."

"Well, I..."

"I am correct in my thinking, Jim?"

"Well, I.."

"I might as well invite you to my bed. Come here to me and take a closer look at what I have to offer you."

"Beth, I don't think we should..."

"Jim, what were you thinking when the breeze lifted my dress this afternoon?"

"Well, I.."

"Jim, you wished you could see more; you wished you could explore what else I had under my dress? I know men, Jim."

"I Guess you are correct, Beth."

"Place your arms around my waist and place your hands on my ass."

"Beth, you don't know what you are asking for."

"Jim, I do know what I am asking for. I am looking for a one-night stand with you and I want you to explore my body fully while I ready myself."

"Ready yourself for what, Beth?"

"Come on Jim, isn't it your intention to fuck me?"

"You might not like it, Beth. I am quite rough in handling a female."

"I can handle it, Jim. Now twist my nipples with your fingers and then place one of those fingers in my crease and massage; make me scream!"

"Beth, lay down on your stomach. I want to gaze at your ass I got a glimpse of. It is as soft as I envisioned."

"Slap me harder, Jim! Make my ass red with warmth!"

"Beth, I can no longer abstain!"

"Go ahead, spread my cheeks and sink that large cock of yours into me. Push hard, Jim, I want to feel you hit the end of my love tunnel."

"Quiet, Beth, I think I heard something."

"Jim, this isn't the time for us to be quiet."

"Shh..."

"Jim, I think you are hearing things in this old castle."

"Beth, sit tight. Don't move from that position. I need to check it out."

"Hurry, Jim. We have been in foreplay most of the night and soon it will be dawn. We have to get to fucking!"

"Who the hell are you and how did you get in here?"

"My name is Jim Faust, and I didn't get out in time before they closed the doors and locked them: I spent the night. I have a ticket. I was touring the castle."

"I am the night watchman and no one is to be in the castle after touring hours."

"Sir, I tried to leave but they locked the doors."

"Are you the only one in the castle? Is there anyone with you?"

"No sir, I am the only one."

"Well, Jim, you look a little disheveled. Are you sure no one is here with you, like maybe a woman?"

"No sir, I am all alone. I wish there was a woman here, with me."

"I've been there. The hand is not as good as a warm and moist pussy."

"You got that right! Can I leave now?" asks Jim.

"Yes, and be sure to leave the next time there is a fifteen minute call on your next visit."

CONTINUING THE NIGHT

"Jim, who were you talking to down there?" asks Beth.

"It was the night watchman. He was wondering why we were spending the night in the castle."

"Did he leave, Jim?"

"I am not sure, but he unlocked the entrance door so we can leave."

"Can't we stay a little while longer, Jim? We were just in the right mood and I am still aroused! What was that?" asks Beth.

"It sounded like the entrance door lock. I bet he thought we left."

"So we still can't leave!"

"No, Beth, we are still locked in. Now where were we?"

"Come over to me, Jim. Give me your hand…"

"What do you want me to do, Beth?"

"Place your fingers in and rub between my lips. Do you feel the lubrication?"

"Beth, you are teasing me!"

"No, Jim, now lie down on the bed. Yes, that is it, now lie still while I place you in my mouth."

"Beth, careful, I might 'cum/ in your mouth."

"That would be OK with me."

"Yes, but I want to feel inside your love tunnel. Beth! Please stop! Let me…."

"There you go, Jim. How does it feel?"

"You are so deep, Beth!"

"Keep pushing Jim…keep pushing. I want you to thrust into me until you can go no further."

"Beth, it is coming! I can feel my discharge running up my cock!"

"Oh, ah, yes Jim! Empty into me…push…push."

"Beth, it is at the end….oh…oh…ohh.."

"Jim, you must have been holding out just for me. Your discharge is flowing out of me…you had a lot of it!"

"I haven't masturbated in a while, but I almost did after I saw your sweet ass yesterday."

"Jim, run your had in your discharge and massage it onto my breasts and around my nipples. Yes, that's it, now put it on my clit and massage…..oh..oh…Yes! Yes! Jim…Jim…rub harder…I…I..oh..oh…"

"Beth, you are squirting from your pussy!"

"Lick me, Jim! Lick it up!"

"Jim, is your cock still hard?"

"It is now since I have been licking your pussy."

"Fuck me in the ass, Jimmy! Push that fucker into my ass as far as it will go…keep pushing!"

"Grab my nipples and squeeze them and twist them…ah…ah…oh..oh..yes! yes! oh, here I go again!"

"Beth, I am afraid we have made a mess of this quilt. You just let a bunch of whatever it is out of your pussy again!"

"Lick it up, Jim! Turn me over and let me see you lick it up. Now kiss me, Jim! Let me taste the discharge! Stick your tongue on mime! Get some more. Let's drink it up!"

"Beth, I can't stop my body from quivering. I can see your bottom throbbing in a rhythm."

"Jim, I am not finished. Stick a few fingers into me and rub me from within my love tunnel. Push in deep!"

"Beth, as you suck my cock, put my ball sac in your mouth and suck it!"

Beth and I become totally exhausted and we fall asleep; me with my fingers still lodged in her pussy and limp as it is, my cock is still mostly in her mouth between her lips.

THE MARRIAGE PROPOSAL

"Wake up, Beth, my sweetheart. It is dawn and we need to figure a way to get out of here undetected."

"Jim, must we? We need to fuck some more."

"Beth, honey, I am spent. We need to recuperate a bit before we have another round. Have you ever fucked so much?"

"Jim, you are the first one and I am glad you are with me."

"Beth, I want to be with you. I want to spend the rest of my life with you. How can I do that?"

"Go back to New York with me. We can live together in my apartment for a while."

"Beth, I want to marry you!"

"I want to be with you too, Jim. I will be your wife."

"It sounds like the public is starting their tour for the day. Let's blend in with them and get out of here. Beth, when we get back to the mainland, let's go to the park I am staying at," says Jim.

"Too bad we can't return here later tonight and spend another exciting and sexy night in the maid's quarters," says Beth.

"We probably wouldn't be able to pull it off again, but it is worth a try," says Jim.

"That is OK, Jim. I want to get married right away."

THE WEDDING

"Sir, my name is Jim Faust, and this is my partner Beth Ridley, and we would like to marry."

"Ok, you will need a certificate to prove neither of you are currently married to someone else, rings and one hundred fifty dollars. If you can get these by tomorrow, I will have you married by the end of day."

"I have the certificate and the rings. When would you like the cash?" asks Jim.

"Let's get started. We are here to witness the marriage of Jim Faust and Beth Ridley in Holy Matrimony."

"Jim Fast, do you take Beth to be your lawfully wedded wife to have and to hold in sickness and health, richer or poorer for the rest of your life until death do you part?"

"I do."

"Beth Ridley, do you take Jim to be your lawfully wedded husband to have and to hold in sickness and health, richer or poorer for the rest of your life until death do you part?"

"I do."

"By the grace of God, I pronounce you man and wife. You may kiss the bride."

"Beth, twist your tongue around mine," says Jim in a whisper.

"Make it a long one, Jim."

"Hmm…would you two like to come up for air?"

"Sorry, sir, let me pay you for your services and we will be on our way to wedding bliss!" exclaims Jim.

13

NO! NO! NOT NOW!

"What's the matter, Jim?" asks Beth.

"I seemed to have misplaced the money. I thought I put it in this pocket."

"Try the other pocket, Jim. With all the excitement, you probably just got confused which pocket it is in," states Beth.

"Oh, here it is……twenty-twenty?" Jim says to himself in utter terror.

"What is it, honey? Jim, what is the matter?" Beth asks with anticipation.

"Oh, Beth! Oh, Beth! No! No! It can't be!" exclaims Jim.

"Jim! Jim! Jim!….Ji…" Beth's voice dissipates into the air.

JIM MIGHT DIE

"Have you seen your brother Jim lately?" asks John.

"No, I haven't. Why, what is wrong?" asks Terri.

"Well, he hasn't been to work since Tuesday and it being Friday, I am worried something might be wrong," says John.

"He came here Monday night, hardly said anything to me and then retired to his bedroom. He looked very stressed," says Terri.

"Let's look in his bedroom. Maybe there is a clue in there to where he might have gone," suggests John.

"Ah.....," screams Terri.

"What is the...oh my God, he is dehydrated!" exclaims John.

"It looks as if he has been lying on his bed for several days!" exclaims Terri.

"Yes, Tuesday till now," says John.

"Is he alive, John?"

"His pulse is very weak," says John.

"Doctor, how is Jim? Will he live?" asks Terri.

"I am not sure. He seems to be in a sub-conscious state. His body is completely dehydrated, and it appears he hasn't eaten for several days."

"Doctor, what happened to him? Why is he in this state?" asks Terri.

"I don't know. I have seen no one so, well, worn out as much as he is. It is like he has spent all of his energy and completely exhausted to a point of death."

"I am going to call his physiologist Mr. Rockner. He has to see this," says Terri.

MR. ROCKNER'S EXPLANATION

"Mr. Rockner, have you seen Jim?" asks Terri.

"Yes, I have. He is very unwell."

"What is the matter with him? How did he get this way?" asks Terri.

"I warned him! I warned him not to push his dream to the extent he has," says the Mr. Rockner.

"What do you mean, Mr. Rockner?" asks Terri.

"Do you remember when this all started with Jim's encounter with the young girl whose dress blew up because of the wind that day when he was on vacation?"

"Yes, I do. That was the beginning of when he came to you because he couldn't get the vision of that girls' bare butt out of his mind," says Terri.

"That is right. He came to me and wanted to extend his dreams, the dreams of seeing her nudity; he wanted to move to the future that didn't exist. He never met her in reality, but he wanted to meet her in his dream and go even further in having a relationship with her."

"How could he do that?" asks Terri.

"I helped him with a certain hypnotism which would allow him to have a genuine dream, allowing him to relive the scene anytime he wanted in a virtual reality. A dream where he could almost reach out and touch her and have a conversation with her. I thought it would satiate his appetite of his obsession."

"But I don't understand. What happened?" asks Terri.

"He came to me last week, wanting me to give him the ability to extend his virtual reality into a future that didn't exist. He wanted to have a relationship with this young girl. I told him it was not possible, but he insisted that he could do it. I warned him not to try; it might lead to his death."

"Did you tell him how to extend his virtual reality, Mr. Rockner?" asks Terri.

"No, I did not because there isn't a way that I know of."

"Then, I wonder how he did it, if that caused this," says Terri.

"By the looks of him and all of his symptoms show that Jim did pass the boundary to the future," says Mr. Rockner.

JIM VOWS TO GO BACK

"Terri, Mr. Rockner, Jim has come into consciousness. Please keep your conversations with him short. He is very weak," says the doctor.

"Jim, how are you doing? What happened?" asks Terri.

"Mr. Rockner, I did it!" exclaims Jim.

"Did what, Jim?" asks Mr. Rockner.

"I extended my dream to the future with Beth. I married her and then...," says Jim as tears come to his eyes.

"Jim, who is Beth?" asks Terri.

"Beth is my wife," states Jim.

"Jim, might Beth be the young girl you saw on your vacation?" asks Mr. Rockner.

"Yes, she is the one. She is the one I have dreams about and I can extend into the future with her."

"Jim, you can't do this. You almost died and you are in a weakened condition from all of that," says Terri.

"Jim, Terri is right. You cannot push your dream into the future again, or you will die," states Mr. Rockner.

"I must get back to Beth! It is our wedding night! I must get back to her!" exclaims Jim.

"No, Jim, no, please don't! Be happy you got to marry her and had some kind of relationship with her. Leave it to that, Jim," says Terri.

CAN WE STOP HIM?

"John, this is Terri. I won't go into the details now, but you know what Jim did?"

"No, I don't."

"He extended a certain dream of which was reality, into the future which is not reality," says Terri.

"Terri, what the hell are you talking about? I have only heard of such things with hypnotism."

"That is right! I am afraid he will try it again. Mr. Rockner, his psychologist, said that if he does, he will die. It has taken a lot out of Jim."

"How can you stop him, Terri?"

"When he gets out of the hospital, I will need to interrupt his sleep for a while until Mr. Rockner figures a lasting fix."

"Mr. Faust, lights out. Get some rest and I will see you in the morning. Remember, the doctor's orders are for you not to dream about Beth. OK?" asks the nurse.

"Yes ma'm," replies Jim.

JIM REUNITES WITH BETH

"*Beth; the castle; the shuttle; the wind; the breeze; her dress lifting; her plump and perfect ass. Beth; the castle; the shuttle; the wind; the breeze; her dress lifting; her plump and perfect ass. Beth; the castle; the shuttle; the wind; the breeze; her dress lifting; her plump and perfect ass. Beth; the castle; the shuttle; the wind; the breeze; her dress lifting; her plump and perfect ass. Beth; the castle; the shuttle; the wind; the breeze; her dress lifting; her plump and perfect ass...*"

"Jim, where have you been?" asks Beth.

"I don't know, Beth. I must have blacked out for a while."

"It has been two days since our wedding and we haven't had our honeymoon yet," says Beth.

"I tell you what, Beth. I will get tickets to the castle and we will lag so we can get locked in again."

"Oh, Jim, I will love that!"

CONTINUING THE DREAM

Ladies and gentlemen, the castle will close in fifteen minutes. Please make your way to the exit. We will be open tomorrow at ten in the morning.

"Jim, I think they closed the castle!"

"I am sorry, Beth. I got lost getting back here."

"I don't hear anyone and haven't seen an attendant for a while. I think they locked us in."

"Let's go check the entrance door, Beth."

"Just as I thought, Jim, they locked it. Now what do we do?"

"I guess we spend the night here, Beth."

"Where are we gong to sleep and oh no, my work! I won't get back there."

"How about you go up to the maid's quarters and make yourself at home in her bed? I will sleep here, in the parlor," says Jim.

"Jim, are you forgetting, we are husband and wife?"

"Oh yeah. That is right!

"Then, come join me in the maid's quarters and share her bed with me," states Beth.

2 0

THE NIGHT RE-LIVED

"*You might not like it, Beth. I am quite rough in handling a female.*"

"*I can handle it, Jim. Now twist my nipples with your fingers and then place one of those fingers in my crease and massage; make me scream!*"

"*Beth, lay down on your stomach. I want to gaze at your ass I got a glimpse of. It is as soft as I envisioned.*"

"*Slap me harder, Jim! Make my ass red with warmth!*"

"*Beth, I can no longer abstain!*"

"*Go ahead, spread my cheeks and sink that large cock of yours into me. Push hard, Jim, I want to feel you hit the end of my love tunnel.*"

"*Not yet Beth.*"

"*Come over to me, Jim. Give me your hand...*"

"*What do you want me to do, Beth?*"

"*Place your fingers in and rub between my lips. Do you feel the lubrication?*"

"*Beth, you are teasing me!*"

"*No, Jim, now lie down on the bed. Yes, that is it, now lie still while I place you in my mouth.*"

"Beth, careful, I might cum in your mouth."

"That would be OK with me."

"Yes, but I want to feel inside your love tunnel."

"Beth! Please stop! Let me...."

"There you go, Jim. How does it feel?"

"You are so deep, Beth!"

"Keep pushing Jim...keep pushing. I want you to thrust into me until you can gone further."

"Beth, it is coming! I can feel my discharge running up my cock!"

"Oh, ah, yes Jim! Empty into me...push...push."

"Beth, it is at the end....oh...oh...ohh.."

"Jim, you must have been holding out just for me. Your discharge is flowing out of me...you had a lot of it!"

"I haven't masturbated in a while, but I almost did after I saw your sweet ass yesterday."

"Jim, run your had in your discharge and massage it onto my breasts and around my nipples. Yes, that's it, now put it on my clit and massage......oh..oh...Yes! Yes! Jim...Jim...rub harder...I...I..oh..oh..."

"Beth, you are squirting from your pussy!"

"Lick me, Jim! Lick it up!"

"Jim, is your cock still hard?"

"It is now since I have been licking your pussy."

"Fuck me in the ass, Jimmy! Push that fucker into my ass as far as it will go...keep pushing!"

"Grab my nipples and squeeze them and twist them...ah... ah...oh..oh..yes! yes! oh, her I go again!"

"Beth, I am afraid we have made a mess of this quilt. You just let a bunch of whatever it is out of your pussy again!"

"Lick it up, Jim! Turn me over and let me see you lick it up. Now kiss me, Jim! Let me taste the discharge! Stick your tongue on mime! Get some more. Let's drink it up!"

"Beth, I can't stop my body from quivering. I can see your bottom throbbing in a rhythm."

"Jim, I am not finished. Stick a few fingers into me and rub me from within my love tunnel. Push in deep!"

"Beth, as you suck my cock, put my ball sac in your mouth and suck it!"

Beth and I become totally exhausted and we fall asleep; me with my fingers still lodged in her pussy and limp as it is, my cock is still mostly in her mouth between her lips.

"Wake up, Beth, my sweetheart. It is dawn and we need to figure a way to get out of here undetected."

"Jim, must we? We need to fuck some more."

"Beth, honey, I am spent. We need to recuperate a bit before we have another round."

JIM! JIM!

"Jim, I am hungry. Do you think we can find some food here in the castle?"

"The store on the third floor has some snack type things and I don't believe they gate it, Beth."

"Take my hand, Jim. Let's go together."

"Here, Beth, are some chips, an apple and a bottle of water."

"That will have to do, Jim, but when we get out of here, we will have to get a proper breakfast."

"I promise, sweetheart!"

"Jim, we need to put down some money. We don't want to be stealing this stuff!"

"You are right, Beth. Let's see...twenty-twenty?" Jim says to himself in utter terror.

"What is it, honey? Jim, what is the matter?" Beth asks with anticipation.

"Oh, Beth! Oh, Beth! No! No! It can't be!" exclaims Jim.

"Jim! Jim! Jim!....Ji..." Beth's voice dissipates into the air.

22

THE RING

"Doctor, what is it? Is Jim OK?" asks Terri.

"I am afraid I have bad news, Terri. Jim passed last night."

"What? Why? What happened?"

"You know he was in a very weakened condition?" asks the doctor.

"Yes, but it appeared he was on the mend."

"Terri, I think you should notify his wife," says the doctor.

"He doesn't have a wife, doctor."

"I figured he does because of the wedding ring."

"What wedding ring?"

"Come look for yourself."

"Doctor, can I remove it to see if there is an inscription?"

"Sure, you are his sister."

"*I swear all of my love to you, Beth, September 23, 1990,*" Terri repeats as she reads the inscription on the inside of the wedding band.

"He has been married for some thirty years?" asks the doctor.

"No, doctor, I don't understand. He doesn't have a wife and never has had a wife."

23

THE EXPLANATION BASED ON FACT

"Mr. Rockner, I am so glad you are here. Look at this. Jim has a wedding band on his finger. Read the inscription," says Terri.

"This is interesting, Terri. Did you find anything else peculiar?"

"I found this in his pocket."

"What is it, Terri?"

"It is a reminder that he has an appointment with you, October 30, 2020."

"Terri, I have been doing some research on extending dreams, or reliving dreams that never happened in reality. There was a case back in nineteen sixty where a young man dreamed himself into a reality. The dream was based on love. He holed up in a hotel room and chanted until he fell unconscious. It appeared he drifted into a past to meet a young lady he always dreamed he wished he had met when he was a child and she a young woman. He carried on a relationship with her. Just like Jim, he came too, back to reality somewhere in the dream, and described what he had done and where in the past he went to. He, too, needed to go back to his love and when found a week later in his hotel room, he was so weakened he died two days later. Quenched in his hand was a penny dated nineteen-sixty."

"What does this all mean? How does it relate to Jim, Mr. Rockner?"

"My guess, the appointment card brought Jim back to us. He experienced his obsession with the young girl, Beth, thirty years ago. In his dream, he went into the past somewhere around the year ninety-ninety. Somehow he must have glanced at the appointment card and it brought him back to us, the reality. It must have snapped his mind out of the dream. As far as his weakened condition, I attribute that to the forging into the future to make a relationship with Beth. The proof, believe it or not, is the wedding band. I have an idea he might have glanced at the appointment card again and he and his mind couldn't handle it the second time, and it took his life."

"I am not sure I understand, Mr. Rockner," says Terri.

"I am not sure I understand it either, Terri."

24

BETH RIDLEY

"Bethany Ann Ridley, do you take Mark to be your lawfully wedded husband in sickness and health, richer or poorer, till death do you part this day, the nineteenth of October twenty-twenty?"

"I...I..No, I can't! I am sorry."

"Beth, what is wrong? You said you loved me and we agreed to get married," says Mark.

"Well, Mark, it is because of this."

"What? That ring. I see you always wear it on your right hand and never seem to take it off. What about that ring?"

"Here, Mark, read the inscription."

"*I swear all of my love to you, Jim, September 23, 1990,*" Mark repeats as he reads the inscription on the inside of the ring.

"This is a wedding band, Beth!"

"Yes, I guess it is Mark."

"So you were married, or are married to a Jim since nineteen-ninety?"

"I must have married a Jim Faust in that year. If it wasn't for this ring, I would swear it was a dream."

"So, where is he now, thirty years later?"

"I don't know, Mark. It is like this big dream. He just disappeared. It is strange, but I somehow have feelings for him. We must have had a deep relationship for a while as husband and wife. I don't think I can give my heart to someone else as long as I have this strange feeling for this Jim."

 Twenty more years have passed. When one visits the Shady Grove cemetery, and under the oak tree, lies two grave markers, side by side. One reads *James Robert Faust, April 15, 1970 to September 8, 2020,* and the other reads *Bethany Ann Ridley Faust, July 20, 1970 to November 18, 2050.*

"*I notice the door is slightly open and a glimmer of light from the full moon is casting light through the window. As I peer into her room, I see a silhouette of her standing in front of the window as the moon shine glows upon her nude body.*"

ABOUT THE AUTHOR

James Roberts is an emerging author of Action Romance and Crime Thrillers. The reader will experience Erotic Love, Deep Suspense with outcomes, sometimes unfathomable.